The Girl Who Talked In Accents

The Girl Who Talked In Accents

A Young Woman's Life in the 1950s

Stories by
Charlotte Zoë Walker

Leaf & Tendril Books

Cover painting by Zoë Méndez

Special thanks to Rebecca Méndez and Mark Evans for production expertise, and Rachel Méndez for design consultation.

Published by Leaf & Tendril Books, 2020

Copyright 2020 Charlotte Zoë Walker

All rights reserved.

ISBN-978-0-578-79938-4

Other works by Charlotte Zoë Walker

Condor and Hummingbird

My Irish Grandmothers

The Fur-Coats-For-All-The-Ladies Christmas and The Blue Carafe

And numerous other stories and essays

Editor of two books on naturalist John Burroughs published by Syracuse University Press

Sharp Eyes

The Art of Seeing Things

For Roland

*This book is dedicated to my beloved daughters
Rebecca and Rachel,
and my five wonderful grandchildren.*

Introduction

The stories in this collection depict moments in the life of a girl who is in her teens in the early 1950s, and a college student a short while later. As her father is in the U.S. Navy, Valerie is accustomed to being the "new girl in school" whenever he is assigned to a new location. One of her ways of surviving is through her sense of adventure, but most of all, her love of books and poetry. Though the stories take place so long ago, I hope that they may convey a little of what life can be like for children whose parents are in the military service, as well as a sense of teen-age life in the 1950s for a shy girl who loves to read.

Contents

13 The Dragon Tea Set

23 The Girl Who Talked in Accents

35 Raymond's Song

47 The Martian and The Librarian

57 What Larks!

69 A Red Jeep

THE DRAGON TEA SET

It was 1952, and Valerie's Dad was just back from the Korean War. Valerie didn't always admit it, but just like her mom and her brother and little sister, she really had been scared for him—on an aircraft carrier out in the middle of a war in the Pacific, on the other side of the world.

But now he was home—except that home was somewhere none of them knew. Dad's new orders from the Navy sent him to Virginia, and the whole family was going with him. They were going to make their way there in two separate—well, *missions* you might call them. Two important missions. The first was that Mom and Val's little sister Carrie, who was very sick with asthma, actually took a plane flight from San Diego all the way to Biloxi, Mississippi, where there was a famous clinic for asthmatics. Val and Kevin had never been on an airplane themselves, and were envious when they watched Mom and Carrie make their way up the steps onto the silver plane, shining under the blue San Diego sky. But their own mission was to drive with their Dad, in the old '47 Hudson, all the way to Biloxi, where they would meet up with Mom and Carrie. And from there, on to Virginia—all five of them together.

The drive through Texas had taken forever. More than forever. Kevin and Val were thrilled and relieved to have their Dad home from the sea; but now here they were driving on dry land with him, mile after mile, and their Dad so silent. All of them were missing their Mom, and maybe even missing Carrie. Val's biggest memory of Texas, besides the endlessness of it, was the rag she saw in the shower in one of those awful auto courts that they stayed in. She stooped to pick up the crumpled rag and toss it out of the shower, but when she put her hands on it, it felt smooth and lumpy at the same time—and it croaked! She screamed, and her father and brother came running. Then they all burst into laughter, while Valerie danced around in her towel and Kevin claimed the toad for himself. It was the best time of the whole journey. And Kevin got to keep the toad as a pet the rest of the way to Biloxi. Now the journey was easier for him, because he kept peeking through the pinholes and seeing how his toad was doing, or opening the lid quickly to drop in a fly.

Mile after mile they drove, and everything seemed the same. They would be grateful for the Burma Shave signs that would show up now and then, with their silly rhymes. There would be a row of signs and you had to be quick to catch them and read the whole verse:

A shave
That's real
No cuts to heal
A soothing
Velvet after-feel
Burma-Shave

Their Dad sometimes had a cut when he shaved, and patched it with a little bit of toilet paper. "Dad, why don't you use Burma Shave?" Valerie asked.

"Because that's not what we used in the Navy," he said, and she could tell by his voice that he wasn't in the mood for questions. And still the miles dragged on, and they would torment him with requests to stop for any attraction that caught their eye. There were hand-painted signs for a Snake Farm, that Kevin begged him to stop for, but he wouldn't.

He did finally agree to stop so they could see "Lady the Wonder Horse," and inside a make-shift theater at the end of an old barn, a horse named Lady showed that she could do math problems by stamping her foot. They sat in wooden folding chairs and watched, enchanted.

"What's 2 and 2, Lady?" asked the man who had let them in, a man about Dad's age, but in overalls, with a scruffy mustache and a crumpled little hat on his head. "What's 2 plus 2?" and Lady would stamp her foot four times. She was a pretty golden-brown horse with an intelligent expression, and Val thought that maybe she really could do simple math problems.

But Dad said he thought she was just responding to signals by her trainer. "That's pretty good, though," he said. Dad had grown up on a farm in North Carolina before he joined the Navy, and Val could tell that he enjoyed seeing Lady, whether she really did math or not. And then they got back in the car, and drove on.

How strange it seemed, when they finally drove up to the clinic in Biloxi after all those miles. It was a red brick plantation type building, with a big circular drive in front of it. Mom and Carrie were sitting in lounge chairs out on the big lawn. Mom greeted them with a happy smile and big hugs for each of them. She was as beautiful as always, with her dark brown hair and her smiling green eyes. Carrie was still pale and fragile looking, but with little dots of rosy color in her cheeks, but she seemed happy and a bit stronger than when they last saw her. They had gone to the clinic so that Carrie could take something called "the red medicine," which was known to have arsenic in it. Mom explained that the arsenic was in very, very tiny amounts, and for asthma it was a kind of cure somehow. Still, there was a dramatic feeling among them, that Mom and Dad were allowing Carrie to take poison in the hope of saving her life.

For the rest of the journey, they were all five crowded into the old Hudson, and Val and Kevin had Carrie in between them, so they had to be careful of her and couldn't pinch each other. She often slept, slumped over against Valerie's side in a sweet but sticky sort of way. Poor Kevin had had to set his toad free. He had walked all the way to the back of the clinic, where there was a little brook, and let it go there. So Kevin was almost too sad to fight anyway. Besides, it was nice watching their parents in the front seat, smiling at each other when the car was at a stoplight. Sometimes even while they were driving, Dad would take a quick look over, and just smile at Mom, or she would gaze at him with a loving smile, while he carefully watched the road. It was strange to see him only in civvies, and not wearing his uniform even once on the whole trip. He always looked so tall and handsome in his dark blue uniform with the gold buttons, and the cap with a bit of gold braid on the visor.

After they got to Virginia, Val had to stay in the motel in Arlington with Carrie, while her parents and Kevin went house-hunting. Val was nine years older than Carrie, who was just seven, so she would hold her little sister in her lap and read stories to her. Carrie loved stories—and especially if they had little songs or rhymes in them, that you could sing together at certain parts of the story. Her favorite was the one about the old woman with the teeny tiny teapot that gets stolen, and when she gets it back, the lid is missing—and how she cries out in the night, "Give me back my teeny tiny teapot lid!!" They would call it out together, and Carrie would giggle so hard sometimes that she started coughing and had to have her "sprayer," with the asthma medicine in it.

They had to spend a couple of weeks in the motel, but now at last, they were moving into a pretty red brick house on Columbus Street in Arlington. It was so different from their little stucco house in San Diego. This Virginia House wasn't very big, but it looked stately and colonial, and had a screen porch outside the dining room, where they could have dinner outdoors if they wanted to, or just sit on the lounge chairs and read (that would be Val) or draw (that would be Kevin or Carrie).

The day they moved in, the Navy sent a moving van and a team to unpack all their things for them, just as they had packed everything up back in San Diego. Mom used to joke that the Navy movers were so thorough, once they had even packed up a wastebasket that was full of trash—but this time they didn't do that.

The furniture was unpacked and set in place in each room; and now came the unpacking of treasures that their Dad had brought from his time on the other side of the world. They had opened them first in San Diego, but now it was like opening their presents all over again. Dad had given the most exciting present to her brother Kevin—a beautiful dark blue model of a Corsair, the kind of plane that flew onto and off of Dad's carrier. It had a wind-up propeller, and could actually fly. But Kevin crashed it before they had even left San Diego. Everyone felt sad for him, and especially now, when there was no present to unwrap for him. But Carrie beamed with joy as Mom handed her the beautiful Japanese doll in a red silk kimono, with a delicate ceramic face and shining black hair that seemed to be real. Carrie had cried when it got packed up, and now she hugged Kyoko close. For Val, the most grown-up of presents, and yet just what she wanted was restored to her: a group of three nesting cedar boxes that smelled heavenly; and a set of six little wooden horses in lifelike poses, grazing or looking at the sky, and one of them rolling on his back.

For Mom there were the most treasures of all: a glowing fire-opal ring, a necklace of real pearls, and a set of Noritake china, service for twelve, in a design she loved that had just one acorn on each plate, with a border of slender brown and gold lines around the edge. "Oh, this is perfect!" Mom said when she had first opened it back in San Diego. Dad had described it to her in a letter, and it was just as beautiful as she had hoped.

There was also a dragon tea set that everyone loved except Mom. The background color was a bright blue, and every piece had a fire-breathing dragon on it, full of reds and greens and shining gold beneath the glazing. The dragons were not small and subtle like the acorns, but big and real looking, taking up every bit of space they could find on a saucer or a cup, and even more on the teapot, where the spout took the form of a dragon's head.

Now the moving men were unpacking the china and setting everything in piles on top of the dining room table, while they put the sawdust curls and shredded paper back into the heavy-cardboard barrels they had arrived in. The Noritake looked elegant and stately, so thin that a stack of twelve plates seemed to take up hardly any room at all. It had arrived without a single chip, except for one at the edge of the gravy boat. Mom sighed over that, but said that with a little drip of gravy, no one would ever notice it.

Trouble was, she couldn't hide from Dad that she didn't really like the dragon tea set. The dragons almost seemed to scare her a little, as if they reminded her of the dangers her beloved had just escaped. To Dad, they were probably something wild and exotic that he'd brought from around the world—something adventurous. To Kevin they were just "neat-o" dragons. And to Valerie, they were creatures from fairy tales—magical creatures! To think that her Dad had gone around the world on a gigantic aircraft carrier, fought in wars, done so many amazing things—and even brought dragons home with him.

The man who was unwrapping the china had come to the dragons now, and he kept remarking, as he unwrapped each cup, each saucer: "These are amazing! I never saw anything like this! Dragons on a tea set!" Valerie stole a look at her mother, and could see that Mom didn't like that the man was commenting on their things. Their private things.

But Dad didn't seem to care. "Do you like them?" he asked.

"They're amazing," said the man. He was a little bit plump, and he had a kind face—but also a face that could love dragons.

"Well, they're yours," Dad said. "What did you say your name is?"

"Joe. Joe Benson."

"Well, Joe, you just wrap those back up and take them home with you."

"Are you kidding me?" His voice became softer, and very serious.

"My wife can't stand them," said Dad. "I'd love for you to enjoy them."

"But Dad," Val whispered urgently, standing right next to him, "I love that tea set!" It was as if he didn't even hear her.

"Only if you're sure," Joe said, but his face was full of happiness already.

"I'm sure," Dad said. It was clear that Joe could hardly believe his luck. He found a cardboard box, and quickly rewrapped the dragon tea set, and placed all the pieces in the box, marked his own initials on it, J.G.B., and took it out to the truck. Val wondered what the G was for. Gregory maybe. Good Luck, maybe. Joe Goodluck Benson! Because he was going home with their dragon tea set! But first he came back, and finished unpacking everything else, while Mom was silently putting pans in the pan cupboards, and glasses in the cupboard nearest the kitchen sink, and so on.

Val was a little angry with her, though she could also see that it wasn't all Mom's fault, that maybe Dad wasn't being fair, when he gave away the tea set, and maybe Mom was even a little bit hurt by it. Still, why couldn't she have liked the dragons? Or at least pretended to like them? Everyone knew that Dad was extra sensitive. That even though he was in the Navy, his feelings could be hurt so easily. She and her brother liked to tease him sometimes, and called him "Popcorn," or laughed when he couldn't make the slide projector work. Then they would feel sorry, because you could see that he was hurt, as he kept getting the slides upside down by mistake—a man who guided airplanes safely onto the deck of a carrier. A man who was brave and heroic when he was far from home, and maybe was just too tired to figure out a slide projector while he rested up at home. What was wrong with them all?

She thought about his aircraft carrier far off in the South Pacific. The carrier itself was named after an ocean; it was called *The Philippine Sea*, and her Dad had been away on it for a year and a half without seeing them once.

Mom had sent him a letter every day, and lots of times Val and Kevin and Carrie added little notes to the letters too. What must it have been like out there? What was war like? Her father used to tell her about flying fishes and dolphins that cavorted in front of him when he had the midnight watch. But he never told her about war.

She wondered—was that what her Mom hated about the dragons? Did they remind her of war? For Val it was easier. She knew that dragons meant fairy tales, magic, medieval castles and villages. Dragons could be scary, but there was nothing wrong with them if you could keep them under control—in a story, or on a tea set maybe.

She supposed the question was this: If you had to choose between dragons and acorns, which would you choose? Her mom chose acorns—and that made sense, because she was making sure they all grew up safe and sound. But Valerie could choose dragons, and that's what she did. And her Dad brought dragons home from the sea.

THE GIRL WHO TALKED IN ACCENTS

"Pip pip, old chap," Valerie said to her brother with a wink, and elbowed him in the ribs. They were in the back seat together again, on their way home from the new shopping center.

"Mom, make her stop!" yelled Kevin.

"Never mind, Kevin," said their mother. "She just likes to talk in accents."

"But she poked me in the ribs too," he protested.

"Valerie," said her Mom, "aren't you too old for that?"

And of course, she was. She was sixteen, in fact, almost grown up. But when it comes to little brothers—especially cute little red-headed brothers that everyone likes better than you—old habits die hard.

"Sorry, Mom," said Valerie. "But if I don't poke, can I still talk in accents?"

"Not if it's just to annoy your brother," Mom said firmly.

"Vot iff it iss to learn a new lengvich?" asked Val—and even Kevin giggled.

"And what language would that be?" asked Dad, who they had almost forgotten was there, silently driving. They had been so glad when he got safely home from the Korean War—but now he was often quiet and a little grumpy.

"I dunno. Hungarian maybe?"

"Maybe you should just stick to English," said Dad.

There was a surprising sternness in his voice, and Val knew she was pushing it when she answered, "Quite right, Pa-pah!"

"American English!" he corrected. "You are American, and ought to be proud of it."

"I am, Dad," she said. "But your Dad came from England, so isn't it okay to do an English accent?"

"I can't remember how my father sounded," Dad said. "I lost him so long ago. But I'm pretty sure he never said 'Pip Pip, old chap' in his life."

They were just on their way home from the big new shopping center in Arlington, and both Val and Kevin had new school clothes in elegant shopping bags from Bullocks. Val was in love with the red and beige plaid skirt her Mom and she had found, and the beige sweater that went with it, and the white blouse with a Peter Pan collar to be worn underneath. For once, she thought, she was going to be wearing the right thing at school. She was grateful to her mother, and had to admit she really was too old to be tormenting Kevin that way. But he was so annoying!

Inside her head she was speaking in a French accent, but she didn't let herself say it out loud. "I lovvv zis café, she declaimed to herself, "Anuzzer croissant, s'il vous plait!"

"Dad," she said out loud—"Doesn't the Navy ever station people in France—or England? I would so love to see where your father was from."

"Very seldom," said her father. "More likely it would be Okinawa in the South Pacific, and I'm not dragging all of you to the other side of the world. No telling how it might affect your sister's asthma."

"I would go," she said. "I'd love to travel anywhere!"

"Well, with luck we'll travel back to San Diego before long," her Dad said.

"But I mean, someplace where they speak a different language," she protested.

"What is wrong with your own language?" he asked. And Valerie knew it was time to shut up.

"Nothing," she said. "I want to write poems in it someday."

"Good," said her father. "You should read Tennyson. Tennyson was my father's favorite poet. Mine too."

"I will," she promised meekly.

But he was already quoting, just as he always did when Tennyson came up: "Sunset and evening star, and one clear call for me…" Here it comes, she thought, and here it came, her Dad's voice distant and almost sad: "And may there be no moaning of the bar, When I put out to sea."

She guessed she should be glad that her father had a favorite poet—even if his favorite poem was about dying at sea. But she couldn't help being bored by "Alfred Lord Tennyson," who showed up in her game of "Authors" as an old guy with a huge bushy beard. Ugh! Still, she was curious enough to ask, "What does he mean, 'moaning of the bar'?"

And her Dad explained again, the thing she could never remember. "It's about the sand bar, out at the edge of a harbor, and the noise it makes as the tide or the wake of a ship washes against it."

Sill, she couldn't really visualize it. It was a lot easier to visualize Edna St. Vincent Millay:

All I could see from where I stood
Was three long mountains and a wood;
I turned and looked another way,
And saw three islands in a bay.

That was what Val called poetry. You could *see* that! And the rhythm was perfect. If only she could write something like that someday. But you had to be a sailor to know whatever that moaning of the bar was supposed to sound like.

"I'd like to invite you all to lunch on my old ship," Dad said to the family one evening. He had been on the *Arctic* since as early as Val could remember. They used to go down to the pier when his ship came in and watch all the sailors pouring off the ship into the arms of their wives and families. Kevin was so little then, he thought every hat was his Daddy's, and when he learned it was only the hat that was like Daddy's he would call out "Daddy's hat! Daddy's hat!" until everyone was overcome by his cuteness—as usual!

Now Dad had mostly shore duty, but the *Arctic* was harbored nearby, and the current captain would gladly welcome them Dad said. So they all put on their best clothes. Valerie wore the green plaid taffeta dress that Mom had bought for when she got invited to parties— which never happened, of course.

When the bosun's whistle piped them aboard, and her dress made that delicious swishing noise as they walked up the gangplank, she felt very grand—like a real lady, not just an officer's daughter. At that moment, the officer's daughter felt quite important, though. They walked through the narrow gray passages of the ship, rivets and turrets and twists-and-turns everywhere—as if it was some newfangled sort of castle, Valerie thought.

The captain greeted her Dad, who looked so handsome in his navy blue uniform with the gold buttons and gold braid. Then Dad introduced the family, and the captain welcomed them all aboard. Kevin's unruly red hair was slicked down with something shiny, but the curls were already starting to spring up again. Their Mom, with her dark brown hair in a pompadour, fluffed around her forehead and tucked behind her ears, looked beautiful in her black silk jersey dress with the sequin appliqué of cascading flowers, and Valerie just hoped Carrie wouldn't spill soup on her or throw up on her or something. She remembered how Mom's other favorite dress had been ruined when Carrie's asthma medicine spilled on it and left a stain. But Carrie was looking adorable in a white organdy dress and pink pinafore, and she was holding tight to their mother's hand, a big smile on her face.

Sailors in dress whites stood at attention near the officer's wardroom, saluting as they were ushered in and led around a long white table, with gleaming silver and shining white plates. Valerie felt embarrassed. It's only us!, she wanted to say. But her green plaid taffeta swished and brushed against some of the sailors as she walked by in the narrow space, and she couldn't help feeling a little bit elegant too. Some stewards from the Philippines, in special waiters' outfits that were different from the sailor uniforms, pulled out their chairs for them.

Soon they were eating a sumptuous dinner, roast chicken and mashed potatoes with a delicious gravy, and tender green beans, cooked just right. Valerie looked up and saw one of the youngest officers looking at her in a shy sort of interested way. She was pretty sure that no one saw it but her, but it made her want to show off just a little.

"Ziss is soch a vunderful deener," she announced as elegantly as she could. "Tres deliceux!"

Her father looked at her sternly, but he didn't say anything. Nobody said anything. The young officer smiled slightly at her, but she could see he didn't dare come to her defense.

On the way home, Dad scolded her, of course. "What was that? Aren't you proud to be an American? Isn't that enough for you?"

"I'm sorry, Dad," she said. But really, she didn't see why she should be. What was so wrong with loving other languages? Her Dad had traveled around the world many times, and must have heard all kinds of languages! Her social studies teacher had told her there is something called The Foreign Service, and that maybe she could find a career there someday. So she tried that on her Dad. "I'm just hoping to join the Foreign Service someday, and be an ambassador," she said.

"Well, believe me, he said, "no one in the diplomatic corps would ever mock the accents of the country they are visiting."

"It isn't mocking," she protested. "I just love the sound of the different ways people talk."

"Well, they're not going to hear it that way," he said.

Valerie shivered. She couldn't believe how her father could know that. Did someone from her high school call and tell him? How could he know? There was a new girl in her social studies class—not Valerie, for once, but *another* new girl. Her name was Amrita, and she actually wore a sari to school—a long, beautiful silk dress in a different colorful pattern each day it seemed, that wrapped around her in a beautiful draping way, and when she bent over you could see her midriff. It was a strange costume to wear to school! You would think that there would be someone who could buy her a red plaid skirt and a blouse with a Peter Pan collar like Valerie's. But no—she wore that sari as if she was still in India. And she wore a red dot right in the middle of her forehead, so mysterious and pretty, somehow!

Some people said that Amrita's father was the new ambassador from India. So her father was in India's foreign service! Valerie was surprised Miss Keck didn't point that out in class, but she supposed it might embarrass Amrita.

Valerie loved to hear the way Amrita talked, and she tried to figure out what it was about an Indian accent that was different from an English accent, which she had mostly heard in movies. It was the same, but not quite—there was something actually more elegant in the way Indians spoke, something proud—even though they had only been a country for a few years. Miss Keck did tell the class about that. She actually gave them a unit on India, and how it became a free country in 1948—only four years ago. Even that seemed dangerously close to embarrassing Amrita, Val thought. But Amrita didn't mind, as far as Val could tell. She would just nod and smile sometimes as Miss Keck spoke.

At lunch one day, Val felt brave enough to sit down next to Amrita, who smiled at her in a welcoming way. "How do you like Miss Keck's class?" Val asked her.

"It's all right," Amrita said. She had a little tin box, and was eating curry from it, with a small wooden spoon. It looked so much more interesting than the sloppy joe on Valerie's tray.

"Youah cuh-ry looks quite excellently delicious," said Val, in her best attempt to sound like Amrita.

"You mock me," said Amrita. "It isn't kind!"

"Oh, I didn't mean to," said Val. 'Really! I just find myself trying to speak in accents sometime—I just love sounds and voices."

"You have to be careful," said Amrita. "It is easy to hurt people's feelings." She snapped the lid on her little tin box very firmly, tucked it in a green-and-gold paisley bag, then stood up and walked away without another word. Val sat there, stunned. She tried to be nonchalant, and finish her sloppy joe, but she felt like an idiot. Lunch time at school was always miserable. The big clock on the wall at the end of the room moved horribly slowly. No one sat down at her end of the table. The noisy chatter of other people,

people who liked each other, went on and on, echoing all around the lunch room. Valerie pulled a book out of her bag and did her best to get lost in it.

So how did her Dad know about that, about how she had offended Amrita and maybe caused an international crisis? Who could have told him? Maybe her Dad met the Indian ambassador at some official event, and the ambassador told him how his daughter Amrita's feelings had been hurt. No. That couldn't be. Maybe Dad was just super smart. He was actually right way too many times.

One day, the social studies class had a field trip to the Library of Congress. They all filed onto a bus, and were driven into Washington, D.C. Valerie was sitting by herself, as usual—when Amrita sat down beside her. Val hardly dared to breathe, for fear she would scare her off. "At least you are interested in things," said Amrita.

"I really didn't mean to offend you before," said Val.

"I know," said Amrita. And then after a little silence, she asked, "What is this Library of Congress we are going to?

"It's where they keep all the books ever published," said Valerie. "Or something like that."

"Do you think they have books in *my* language?"

"I don't even know what your language is," Valerie admitted.

"It's called Hindi," Amrita said.

"Well, I bet they have something."

Soon the bus let the class off on the Washington Mall, where Valerie's family had sat on a blanket on the lawn for fireworks on the Fourth of July. It set them down in front of an imposing stone building, with a huge, wide set of stairs leading up to the entrance.

It looked pretty much like all the other big government buildings in one way or another. Except when they got inside! Miss Keck led them on a tour through shining marble corridors—beautiful marble tiles gleaming under their feet, and white marble columns along the sides. From a high marble gallery, Miss Keck had them look down—and there was the most magnificent place Valerie had ever seen.

"*That* is the main Reading Room," Miss Keck said in a hushed voice. It was astonishing. Like a temple or a sacred place, dedicated to books. They were standing at the balustrade of a circular gallery, above a gigantic round room, with a high dome over their heads. Several different galleries ran in circles beneath the dome. Looking across the space, Val could see that the gallery just above them had statues on it—but they were too far away for Valerie to guess whether they were poets or politicians.

At the center of the carpeted floor below them was a huge round desk, where librarians were working silently, or helping people. And then, in expanding circles around the central desk were curving semi-circles of desks for people to sit at.

"We're going down there next," Miss Keck told them. "But you *must* be very quiet there. And if you like, each of you can order a book of your own choosing just like the scholars who do research here."

She sat them down in one section—all fifteen of them—and told them that they could each order a book if they liked. Some of the boys joked about ordering Superman comic books or pinup magazines, but Valerie knew right away that she'd order something by Edna St. Vincent Millay. "What are you ordering?" She whispered to Amrita.

"You'll see," she whispered back.

After they looked at the card catalogs and wrote down their requests, they sat back at their desks and waited. And waited. Finally, the books began arriving in square wire baskets that almost-invisible librarians brought to their tables.

A Few Figs from Thistles, by Edna St. Vincent Millay, a thin little book with a dark blue cover, sat in its basket, waiting to be picked up. But Valerie was distracted by Amrita's books. She watched as Amrita reached into the basket with her delicate hands and brought out a book printed in a strange red binding such as Valerie had never seen before—some kind of rough cloth stretched over very thin, bendy boards. Valerie couldn't read the title, for it was written in strange looking squiggles.

"What IS it? She asked in a hushed voice.

"*The Bhagavad Gita*," said Amrita. It is a very sacred book in my country. It's in Sanskrit—the oldest language in the world, my Papa told me. He says that Hindi and Sanskrit and English all come from the same early language."

"You mean my language and yours are connected?"

Amrita nodded.

"That's amazing," said Valerie. "It's almost like poetry, just to think that!"

"Isn't it?" said Amrita.

"But those letters are so different! How do you read them?" Val asked. "I can't even make out how you would pronounce them."

"To me they are beautiful," said Amrita. And she read a few phrases, in a very soft voice.

It *was* poetry! It clearly was poetry.

"Look," said Amrita, pulling another book from the basket. "Here it is in English—and also the Sanskrit words so that you can read how they sound. 'Sanjaya uvacha, dristva tu pandavanikam'—"

"Oh, let me try," said Valerie, grabbing the book. "Sann-jayy-a yuh-vatch—"

"Oh, Valerie," Amrita smiled at her, her lovely dark eyes brimming with laughter. "Your accent is *dreadful!*"

RAYMOND'S SONG

She was tired of being the new girl in school. This big high school in Arlington wasn't the worst Valerie had been to; it might even be the best school in Virginia. But the Navy was sure to give her Dad new orders and move them along again in a year, or even just a few months. Her Mom had made a list for her: It was 1952 and only her junior year—and she had already been to 14 schools. There was no point in trying to make friends. Nobody ever liked the new girl anyway. Except for that other Navy brat, Miranda, who was so sure of herself and had that amazing haircut, and who had just come back from China. Everyone thought Miranda was interesting. But Valerie's Dad had never been stationed anywhere exciting, and she had no idea where you could get a haircut like that.

Val had decided to be a poet instead. And to be a poet, she needed the secretary desk she had seen in a furniture store when her parents were shopping for a new dining set. It had a drop-down writing desk with little niches inside for envelopes and sealing wax and pens; and a bookcase above, with glass doors that protected your books of poems, and where a poet could see her own reflection by candlelight. It looked just like the one she had seen in a book about William Wordsworth, who wrote "I wandered lonely as a cloud," and first made her love poetry. "A host of golden daffodils!" She was sure her favorite women poets must have had such a desk too, though she had seen no pictures to prove it.

Her parents encouraged initiative, and so they said yes to her idea of earning money for the secretary by getting a job in the shopping center in Arlington, just a short bus ride from home. From poetry to commerce! But that didn't bother Valerie. It was all an adventure. To her surprise, the first place she applied to—the pretty little Fannie Farmer candy store, with its bright white interior and checkerboard tile floor—accepted her immediately.

Fran, the woman who hired her, was tall and thin with a stern face and short, tightly curled brown hair. She was a stern manager too, a stickler for being on time and wearing one's hairnet properly. But May, the full-time sales clerk was round and gentle, with cheeks that jiggled a bit, and a warm laugh. It was May who told Val she should sample the chocolates freely, so that she could describe them to customers and answer their questions. "Of course," she added, "you might gain a pound or two—but it's worth it to be well informed."

The stock boy, Raymond, was seventeen, just like Valerie, and they took a quick liking to each other. He knew where all the various styles and flavors of chocolates were kept—the nougats, the creams, the cordials—and when Val was sent back to refill the counter trays or get some extra candy boxes, Raymond would nimbly find just what was needed. He was a slender, handsome boy; his skin was as dark as the darkest of the chocolates, and his smile as lovely and sweet. He often wore a dark blue sweater with a blue plaid shirt beneath it, under his white Fanny Farmer apron, just like the apron Valerie wore behind the counter.

For some reason Valerie didn't feel shy with him, the way she did with the kids at school. Raymond was so easy to talk with. They would chat as they worked together on the margins between stock room and candy shop, and sometimes during their lunch breaks on Saturdays, Valerie would find a stool in the stockroom and sit there, with her new, pleated plaid skirt spread comfortably over her knees under the white apron. She would sit there so happily and eat her sandwich while Raymond, on another stool, ate his. He laughed at her pickles-and-peanut butter sandwich and told her she must be crazy, and then she laughed too.

"My brother invented it," she said. "You should try it. Here!" and she tore off a quarter of her sandwich.

He accepted the proffered section, but held it up doubtfully, a comic frown on his face. "I don't know... no telling what it might do to me."

"Just see," she urged.

"Peanut butter. Pickles. Okay, here goes!" He chewed slowly and carefully.

"Good, isn't it?"

"Not bad," he said. "But you can't beat my mom's baloney sandwich with mayo and lettuce."

His eyes were bright and friendly in his dark face, in the dim stockroom with one bright doorway into the sales room, and one leading to the alley way behind—and the walls full of shelves in between.

Once Val got to work ten minutes late, and had to explain to Fran that her little sister had just had a serious asthma attack. She was afraid to leave the house until she knew Carrie was okay.

"I understand," Fran said. "But please don't let it happen again."

A little later, during the afternoon lull, Raymond asked her, "Your little sister has asthma?"

"Yes. It's really bad. Sometimes I just want to get away from home because my parents are always so worried."

"My mom and my little brother have it too." "Oh, I'm sorry! It's awful, isn't it?"

"Yeah, That's why I have this job. I try to help out so my mom won't have to work so much. It's not good for her."

"What kind of work does she do?"

"Takes in laundry. But you know, all the clothes, they're kind of dusty—sometimes they can make her wheeze."

"I hate asthma! I have it too, and so does my brother—but we try to push back, push it away."

"Me too," said Raymond thoughtfully. "I kind of push it away too. I think about fishing, how nice it is by a slow river, just fishing. And then I start to breathe better."

"That's what my brother does! He does the same thing, he just goes fishing! My Mom drops him off at a fishing spot and he'll just stay there all day."

"I bet I'd like your brother. Bet I could show him some good fishing spots."

"Bet he could show you some too."

"I bet he could." Both of them were grinning at each other, then broke out laughing.

Fran stepped into the stock room. "What's going on here?" Raymond jumped up from his stool and stood respectfully.

"Just talking during lunch," Valerie said. She stood up and brushed the crumbs from her skirt.

"Sorry, Ma'am," said Raymond.

"You both know better," Fran said. "Customers can't come into our shop and hear that kind of noise. Lunch is over. Now get back to work. And Valerie–from now on, when you do a full day here you are to take your lunch away from the store."

"But why?" Valerie asked.

"You know very well why," said Fran. "Now go check the stock in the display cases."

So Val started having her lunch at the Howard Johnson's, just a short walk down the street. She sat at the end of the orange Formica counter and ordered the fried egg sandwich with mayo, on a soft roll. It tasted really good, and she thought how Raymond would like it too. But she looked around, and there was no one like Raymond in the Howard Johnson's. She guessed it was like the school buses that had shocked her so much when she moved to Virginia–how all the white kids rode on one school bus, and all the colored kids on another one, going in the opposite direction. She asked her seat mate

Erin, who was also a Navy brat, what that meant; and Erin told her it was called segregation. So that's what all of this was about, she supposed. Was there a separate Howard Johnson's too? And another Fanny Farmer's where Raymond was in the front of the store, and she was in the back?

Before long, Val and Raymond forgot about Fran's rules. They couldn't help it. Val couldn't have lunch in the stock room any more, but she still had to go back to pick up new supplies for the display cases. And sometimes, when there were no customers, she would just stand at the edge of the counter, and talk to Raymond, who was just inside the stockroom door. They would chatter back and forth between their designated places, like neighbors being neighborly over a backyard fence. Nothing wrong with that, they thought.

Sometimes they would talk about music. The Mills Brothers' "Glow Worm" was high on the charts just then, and Raymond told her that he wanted to write a song like that someday.

"You want to write songs?"

"Yeah."

"I want to write poems," she confided.

"Neat," he said. "A poem–isn't that just a song waiting for its music?"

"Maybe. I love that. Only some of my poems don't rhyme. They wouldn't make very good songs. Like–I just wrote one about a Cheetah that's got really short lines... because, you know, it's the fastest animal in the world."

"Hey, a song can have short lines too! "Glow little Glow Worm!" Grinning, he bobbed his head in rhythm and she bobbed hers back at him. Together they chanted the rest: "Glimmer!"
"Glimmer!"
How could they not be laughing?
Next time Val came in to work, May was on duty in the front of the shop. Usually she worked on May's days off, but today May was here. And it was kindly May who whispered to her while Fran was still in back, "Raymond's been fired."
Val looked at her in alarm, and May squeezed her shoulder, gave a sad shake of her head. Then Fran came in from the stock room, her arms full of empty, shiny white Fanny Farmer boxes, her face a frown above it.
"I see May's told you," she said. "It's your own doing. If you'd taken my warning and not acted like a floozy with him, Raymond would still have his job. Here. Put these in the cupboard." She slid the pile of boxes into Valerie's arms.
Floozy. No one had ever called her that. She had barely even ever heard the word. The boxes were very lightweight, but she slid to the floor as if they were bricks. She slid open the cabinet under the display counter, and began putting the boxes away, one by one. She was so close to the neat rows of chocolates in the display case that their sweet, rich scent made her feel dizzy, almost nauseous.
When she was able to stand up, she looked straight at Fran: "Why didn't you fire *me* instead?"
"Raymond should have known better."

"We just liked to talk," Val said.

"It made a very bad impression," said Fran. She spoke sharply—but didn't she also seem a little embarrassed? Her eyes glanced to one side and then the other—but not back into Valerie's.

Val knew she had to quit. But she didn't think she could put the words together then.

Just two words, just "I quit," but she couldn't say anything, not anything. Three customers came in, two middle-aged women together, buying a treat for themselves; and a happy-looking man who wanted a present for his girlfriend. The man smiled at Val and asked her to put together the best selection, the very best creams and maybe just one or two nougats. She made sure his sweetheart got the maple cream and the apricot cordial—her own favorites. The women took forever, just picking out a dainty white paper bag for each of them, three chocolates each.

Val went home that night full of sadness, but she couldn't tell anyone. What was there to tell? She was so ashamed that she got Raymond fired, and what could her parents tell her? That it was her fault. And they would be right.

"I think I'm going to switch jobs," she told them at dinner.

"Really?" said her Dad. "I thought you liked it there."

"I did, but—I think I gained weight eating all that candy."

"Ha ha, Round Valerie," chuckled her brother. She scowled at him.

"!" said their Mom.

"It's okay," Val said. "It's true. I think maybe I'll try the Woolworth's across the street. I'm getting close to enough money for my secretary desk—and then I can quit and catch up on my homework."

"Never neglect your homework," Dad said. "That's a lot more important than a stick of furniture."

So nobody in her family knew about Raymond, and how she caused him harm. And she couldn't tell them. All she could do was go across the street and apply at Woolworth's. It was an awful place, with a grubby employee's room and a time-stamp machine that you stuck your card into when you came in and when you left, and it made a sharp little noise. It told exactly if you were two or three minutes late, and they would nag at you and warn you about that.

They put her to work in Notions, where a craggy-faced man named Mr. Dugan was in charge. He had dandruff in his hair, and he kept touching her hand as he showed her how to handle the many-colored spools of thread and place them on their little wooden dowels. She stepped back whenever he came close to her, but still whenever she was at work, she could feel him watching her with a disgusting look on his face. She would look away, but still she could feel that look, as if a snail was walking over her and leaving a trail of slime. That's how she thought about it, but she was so close to enough money for her desk now—if she stuck it out for three weeks, the desk of a poet would be hers.

One day, she saw Mr. Dugan frowning at an African American woman who was looking at the embroidery threads. Val quickly rushed up to wait on her. "Can I help you?" she asked. Then she saw the tall boy standing next to the woman, taller than she was. He had on the dark blue sweater and the blue plaid shirt that he used to wear to work at Fanny Farmer's underneath the white apron; only now he didn't have the apron.

"Raymond!" She said.

"Hi," he said quietly.

"Is this your Mom?"

"Yeah. Mama, this is... my friend Val."

"Pleased to meet you, Ma'am," Valerie said. You could tell she was Raymond's mother. She had the same high cheekbones he did, and she must have been very beautiful once. But now she just looked tired, and her face seemed sad. Val remembered how Raymond said she was often sick with asthma.

Raymond's mother nodded at her with a brief half-smile, then turned to Raymond. "The one who got you fired?"

"It wasn't her fault, Mama," he said.

"We have to be careful about our friends in this world," she said. Her face looked very stern to Val. She pushed two small packets of embroidery thread toward Valerie. "I'll take these, please."

Turquoise and a deep glowing orange, colors that Val loved. When she colored with her little sister in Carrie's coloring book, she liked to use those colors together. A turquoise bathrobe for a little chipmunk last time, and orange slippers. Maybe Raymond's mother embroidered flowers, the way her mother did. Turquoise and orange flowers would be nice too.

She rang up the embroidery thread, put it in a little paper bag, the same size as the one's at Fanny Farmer, but brown like a lunch bag—and handed it to Raymond's mother.

"Thank you," Val said, and then she turned to Raymond, her heart bursting. "I'm so sorry."

"It's okay," said Raymond. "I like my new job better."

"I quit, you know. The next day."

But Raymond's mother had turned around, and he was following her. He looked back with a regretful smile, a bit of his old friendly smile in it too. But she couldn't tell if he had heard her.

The day the secretary desk arrived, Val's family seemed to be excited for her. "Looks like you're really going to be a writer!" Said her Dad.

They directed the moving men upstairs to Valerie's room, and her mother helped her to make a space for it, right next to her bed, and even gave her the sixth chair in their dining room set, so she'd have a chair to go with the desk. "We'll have to borrow it back if we invite someone to dinner," her Mom said.

"Of course," said Val. "Thanks, Mom."

And then after dinner, she moved all her papers and her leather-bound diary into the top drawer, and put her special stationery, with the little bar of sealing wax, and the seal with a rose on it for sealing special letters, into two of the little niches inside the desk part. There was a tiny key in a keyhole of the drop-down desk, and she loved turning the key. But she was afraid of losing it, so she didn't take it out, not yet anyway.

The very first night, she sat there by candlelight after reassuring her parents that she would be very careful and she wrote three poems. She looked at her reflection in the glass doors of the bookcase part of the secretary, and it was just as she had dreamed it would be. She looked to herself like a poet, like Emily Dickinson or even her idol, Edna St. Vincent Millay, whose poems flowed so liltingly:
We were very tired, we were very merry—
We had gone back and forth all night on the ferry;
And you ate an apple, and I ate a pear,
From a dozen of each we had bought somewhere ...
Val's eyes were almost hidden in the wavering light, but her hair fell softly around her face, and she could see that her mouth was a poet's mouth. Words were hiding there, but they would come out through her fingers, come out onto paper, they would tell the truth about things. Except that she couldn't write a poem about Raymond. She tried and tried, but she just couldn't. Her hand wouldn't budge, it was just stuck there on the paper and no words would come. She wanted to ask Raymond if he'd heard her say that she quit the job after he was fired. She wanted to tell him that she missed being his friend. But how could you do that in a poem?

All she could think of was a song—and Raymond was the one who wrote songs.

THE MARTIAN AND THE LIBRARIAN

First there was a blissful summer in Virginia Beach, where Val's family lived just two blocks from the ocean. To get out to the breaking waves for body surfing, Val and her brother Kevin had to run fast through the shallow water, where crabs were like a carpet underfoot. Swift though their feet were, they still felt the crabs, like upside down saucers pressing into the sand, claws just grazing their nimbleness. They laughed all the way, and felt wonderfully brave. Their dad was in the Navy, and they had suddenly been placed there by his most recent orders.

Everything was perfect until fall, when Valerie found herself attending Oceana High School, a grim old building that was going to be shut down at the beginning of 1953, as soon as the new school building was finished. Just Val's luck, to get stuck in the old school's final year! Kevin was in a different school, the nearby Junior High, and maybe it was just Kevin–but his school didn't seem to be as bad as Oceana High.

Valerie had one teacher for three of her main classes plus the chaos of study hall. She thought of him as

Mr. Thicktongue, because in French class he announced on the first day that they would study translations, but never pronounce words in French, because he had a thick tongue that prevented his speaking French out loud. This was horrifying to Valerie, whose dream was to live in Paris and have coffee and croissants at a sidewalk cafe. How would she ever learn to speak French, with Mr. Thicktongue for her teacher?

In chemistry class, he told them that the element "I" stood for Iron, when even Val, who was bad at science, knew it was Iodine. In social studies, he loved to rant about how Eleanor Roosevelt could talk all she wanted about the children he called "pickaninnies," but she didn't have to smell them. Val shivered in horror at everything he said, but that class was the worst. It made her feel ashamed and disgusted, and she thought of her friend Raymond, the boy she had worked with at the candy shop in Arlington. They were not allowed to be friends, but still "friend" was how she thought of Raymond. And here was her teacher, talking about people like Raymond in that hateful way. At least it made her love Eleanor Roosevelt and want to learn more about her.

There were also mean kids at Oceana. One day when Val was in a toilet stall in the Girls' Room, reading all the writing on the wall—"Jim + Shirley" with a heart around it, and "I hate Jody Smith," and "You are a cunt," right underneath—she heard, through the chipped wooden door that would barely stay closed, a familiar voice talking by the row of sinks on the opposite wall,

"If I don't get my period soon I'll put a firecracker up my ass!"

What a scary thing to say! Val felt a chill, and her mind went over the few things she knew about periods and sex. She was pretty sure the girl was Evie, in her study hall, who everybody knew because she was a cheer leader for the football team—the Cavaliers. Val hoped she would go away by the time Val flushed and came out to wash her hands.

But no—she was still standing there—the beautiful Evie, with her shiny, shoulder-length brown hair. She was standing there next to her friend, a blond girl whose name Val didn't know—and they were both putting on mascara in front of the mirror with the exact same gestures, swooping up along their eyelashes with their little mascara brushes.

Silently, Val pulled a hair brush from her book bag and began to brush her brown hair that was too short for a pageboy, and always looked a bit rumpled.

"You're so ugly—why do you bother?" Evie said. Val looked into the mirror in shock, and saw that Evie was looking at her, making unfriendly eye contact right in the mirror.

Val didn't say anything. Just shoved her brush into her bag and walked out of the Girls' Room. Maybe she was ugly. It was hard to know, because she didn't have any friends. They moved around so often and she wasn't good at getting to know people. So maybe she was ugly. For sure, she wouldn't take any chances again, she wouldn't brush her hair in the Girls' Room at school. She thought about it the rest of the day. She wondered if maybe Evie just realized that Val had overheard her talk about the firecracker, and was embarrassed. Or maybe she was just mean. Or maybe she was right, and Val really was ugly.

Her brother Kevin had seemed just as miserable in his new school at first—except that Kevin had a gift for making friends, and a way of finding places to go fishing after school, wherever the Navy set them down. Their mother, through all the different moves they made, from one city to another, whenever the Navy relocated them, was always willing to take Kevin to the fishing spot of his choice. And for Val, she always found where the nearest library was, and made sure that the librarian would allow her more than the usual limit of books.

Back in San Diego, Val had been allowed to take a bus after school to the downtown library, a beautiful old building with palm trees in front of it. It would be the happiest moment of the day, walking up the stone steps to the big and welcoming library.

Somehow she had managed to ask one of the San Diego librarians if she could have a volunteer job, and right away they assigned her the job of shelving books, pulling the rubber-wheeled book cart around the library from aisle to aisle. What a pleasure—to read the enticing titles of books she hadn't seen before, and learn to use the Dewey Decimal System to find their proper places on the shelves.

So it was that in Virginia Beach, Val's mother found the little public library, just a few blocks from home. She would drop her off there after school, and then Val would walk home on her own. She just had to be home in time to set the table for dinner.

The Virginia Beach library was nothing like the big libraries in San Diego and Arlington that Val was used to. It was a small wooden building placed sideways on a narrow lot, with a row of windows like a diner might have. It was the sandiest library that Valerie had ever seen. The concrete path to the entry door was always sprinkled with beach sand. There was even a sign at the checkout desk that said, "You are welcome to take library books to the beach–but please be careful of sand and foam! You are responsible for the books you check out."

Just as you might expect, there weren't very many books to choose from at the Virginia Beach Library. Val had read *The Black Stallion* by Walter Farley in Arlington, and was hoping to read *The Island Stallion*–but the library didn't have it. They didn't even have *Sue Barton, Student Nurse* which Val would have been willing to read, even though she wanted to be a poet and not a nurse. Still, it was a library, and Val was free to explore.

She found a book on mountain climbing, and enjoyed reading about the highest mountains in the world. She wondered if, in spite of having some of the family asthma, she could ever become a mountain climber–but she learned from the book that it was harder to breathe in high altitudes. The air was thin, they said–whatever that meant.

The library didn't have any of her favorite poets. She couldn't find anything by Edna St. Vincent Millay or even Wordsworth. There was a book of Rudyard Kipling's poetry, which wasn't what she really loved, but at least it was poetry. And it helped a little, to read "If you can keep your head when those about you are losing theirs," with all its advice on being strong and steady. But when you got to the end, it said that if you could do all that, "you'll be a man, my son." What about her? What about girls? Mom said it really meant her too—that if you could do all that you'd be a strong person, a grownup. But Val didn't think so, and she returned the Kipling before it was due.

Then one day she found *The Martian*. It was probably the most beautiful book in the library, and didn't have a trace of sand between the pages. In fact, when Val looked at the circulation slip at the back of the book, she saw that no one had ever taken it out.

"Oh, you found *The Martian!*" the librarian exclaimed. "That's one of my favorites."

"Really? It looks like no one ever took it out."

"That's because I donated it," said the librarian, Miss Johns. She had a long, friendly face, with a big smile, and her kind face was crinkly with lines and wrinkles. "Did you know, George du Maurier was Daphne du Maurier's grandfather?"

"Who?" asked Valerie. She felt stupid not to know.

"You know, Daphne du Maurier who wrote *Rebecca*, and *My Cousin Rachel*. The ones they made movies of."

"Oh—yes." Val remembered that *My Cousin Rachel* was still in the theater in Arlington, but Mom hadn't let her go see it. Maybe it was because she and Kevin always went together when they went to a matinee, and even though Val was grown up enough, Kevin wasn't. Maybe that was it.

Anyway, now she had *The Martian*, by George du Maurier to look at.

Reverently, Val carried the book home, and took it straight to her room. It had a soft rust-colored fabric cover, with a gilded design on the front. Two irises rose up to surround the title, and underneath the gilded words, *The Martian*, was a golden compass-like design, with the crossed images of an artist's brush and a quill pen. Inside, the book was full of illustrations by the author, lively little black-and-white drawings that Val enjoyed.

But the marvelous thing was the story! It was a story about a man who was a bit different from others, and who received special guidance from a spirit—who just happened to be from Mars. He would fall asleep at night, and when he awoke in the morning there would be a message from "Martia" in his own handwriting! Over the years, Martia not only sent him words of guidance, but gave him all the words for wonderful novels that made him a world famous author. What was even more wonderful was that whole sections of the story took place in France, especially in Paris. If the characters had conversations in French, du Maurier didn't even bother to translate the words to English—so Val had to use her French dictionary and remember what she had learned in her French class in Arlington, before the days of Mr. Thicktongue. It was wonderful. What a joy, to read about Paris, and translate the French phrases all by herself. And what an amazing idea about being a writer—that maybe someone could send you all the words while you were asleep, and then when you woke up, it would all be there, in your own handwriting!

Before her Dad was ordered to Virginia Beach, Valerie had had one blissful school year in Arlington, Virginia, where the teachers were the best teachers she had ever known. There was a social studies class where Miss Francis Keck, told Val that there was something called the Foreign Service in the State Department, and that she might enjoy a career there. For creative writing class there was kindly Mr. Carpenter, who looked like Danny Kaye, and told Valerie that her poems showed talent. And best of all was the French teacher, Mrs. Waters. She taught her first-year French students so many clever rules that being in class was nearly as exciting as a sidewalk cafe in Paris.

"Careful!" she would announce dramatically, as she wrote the word "careful" on the blackboard and with her trusty chalk drew firm little lines under each of the consonants. "C, R, F and L—the only consonants to be pronounced at the ends of French words!" She let them in on secrets like that as if they deserved to know them and would use them well. Even Mr. Thicktongue would have learned French if he'd had the luck to be in class with Mrs. Waters. And if only Valerie could have had another year in Mrs. Waters' class, she might have learned French well enough to live in Paris for the rest of her life.

Instead, like the heroine of a gothic romance written by George du Maurier's granddaughter, Val awoke to find herself in the world of Mr. Thicktongue, in desperate dejection in four of his dreary classes, in the miserable old building that was Oceana High, where one of the cheerleaders was in danger of doing something foolish with a firecracker.

And then—just as suddenly, they were rescued. Dad came home one night in January to say they were moving. He'd asked for a hardship change of orders because Carrie's asthma was worse in Virginia Beach—even Kevin's asthma was worse. And the request had been granted—they were moving back to San Diego!

It was as if a spell had been broken and the family came to life again. How quickly they all pitched in, packing up their own things, helping Mom in the kitchen. They almost didn't need the Navy movers, they were so eager, so ready to go.

And then there was the last trip to the sandy little library near the beach. Valerie gathered up the meager pile of books she had checked out—and right on top, she placed *The Martian*. How could she ever part with it? It had been her companion through the hardest times. She had lain on her bed reading it, with tears pouring down her cheeks, and had used the hem of her blouse to daub the tears away from the creamy old pages. Such a special book, and no one cared about it but her!

After she handed over the other books, Valerie gathered her courage to ask Miss Johns. "Do you think I could buy this one?"

"Buy it? But it's a library book," Miss Johns said.

"I know," said Val. "But if you look at the back—you'll see that nobody ever took it out before. I'm the first person that ever took it out."

"Now that is interesting," said Miss Johns. "When I donated *The Martian* to the library, I certainly hoped that more people would discover it.

"And I think it's been here a long time," said Val. "It was published in 1897."

"Well–not quite that long," said Miss Johns. "But yes–eighteen years, to be exact. But this *is* a library, you know. And maybe in another few years someone else would come along and love it as much as you do, and then it would be right here for them."

"But I have to move again," said Val. "I'm going to be the new girl in school again, and my Mom counted up for me. It's going to be my sixteenth school!"

"That *is* a lot," said Miss Johns. "And how can *The Martian* help with that?"

"I don't know. It's like a friend," said Val. "A friend I can't leave behind. I could pay two dollars for it. I have that much saved."

Miss Johns looked at her seriously. "I couldn't take money for such a thing, she said. "But I am thinking that–considering that in eighteen years nobody else has ever taken *The Martian* out of the library–maybe it does belong with you."

She handed the beautiful, rust covered book with its gilded design and gilded letters back to Valerie.

And that was how she became strong enough for one more move, for being the new girl in school just one last time before she went to college–where everyone in her class would be new, and it would be almost like going to Mars and meeting her true companions.

WHAT LARKS!

Valerie was just finishing her first semester at San Diego State when her father got new orders from the Navy—again! He was to go to Colorado to work with the Naval Reserve there. Whoever heard of ships in the Rocky Mountains? But her Dad was going to be the liaison with the new Air Force Academy. He showed them pictures of its beautiful architectural design. It was 1954, and everything was changing.

The whole family was excited. The Rocky Mountains! It seemed like a dream assignment, and they were all thrilled: her Dad, her Mom, her brother and her little sister. Everyone but Valerie, who was devastated. She had just made friends in school for the first time in her life. It was all because of the Freshman Quad at San Diego State. The kids who didn't want to join fraternities or sororities—the kids who majored in English or Philosophy and liked to read Shakespeare out loud to each other—hung out there, in a hedged-in square with benches in the middle, and a few palm trees at the corners. Valerie loved going to the Frosh Quad between classes and chatting with her friends there. She actually had friends.

And now they wanted her to move to Colorado and start over again?

Her Mom understood. But what could they do? "San Diego State is a streetcar college," Mom said. "There are no dorms. And how could we afford one anyway?"

"There is one girl's dorm," said Valerie. She had been to the dean's office in desperation and done some research. "It's called Quetzal Hall–after the Aztecs–and it's just a half mile from campus. I could walk to class easily. And I can get a part time job.

And so it happened. They left her there, and all four went off happily to Colorado. Val envied their happiness, and felt left out. She suspected that they hadn't really wanted her with them anyway. Now they were a perfect family of four, with one boy and one girl–and no grumpy girl-poet to spoil things.

Quetzal Hall was a drab, two-story concrete building, taller than it was wide, set on a flat, empty dirt lot. The sofas in the downstairs lounge were cracked brown leather, and the girls' rooms upstairs were what you might expect. There was a lot of cabbage in the dinners at Quetzal Hall; the hallways had a permanent, stifling cabbage smell, even when you woke up in the morning. The dorm mother was a cross old woman with a permanently grubby white apron over her vast front. Her pudgy husband, the maintenance man, had a habit of coming upstairs to check the plumbing and sneak a look at the girls *before* calling, "Man on the floor!" as he was supposed to do.

Valerie got a job washing dishes after supper, to help lower the cost for her parents. And her Mom gave her their portable sewing machine, so that she could keep on making her own clothes. She soon learned how you could dry several plates at once by just drying the top and bottom of the stack in your hands, and then sliding the top to the bottom—like a deck of cards. And as for sewing—well, true to the C-minus she got in Home Ec in high school, her skirt waistbands were rounded and lumpy, and her hems were uneven. But she got to choose colors that she loved, like a soft gray and white plaid that she wrote a poem about for creative writing class, called "Serenity is a Gray Dress." Professor Theobald wrote a note on it: "You have a voice of your own." She was thrilled, until Tom Hernandez told her that he wrote the same thing on *his* poems too. "I think he writes it on everyone's poems," Tom told her, a bit apologetically.

She was actually doing better in Philosophy class, where her professor told her she was one of the best students he ever had. But when she said she'd like to major in philosophy, he discouraged her. "It's sad to say," he told her, "but there are no women philosophers. It would be a dead end for you." And since majoring in poetry seemed too good to be true, Val decided to major in Psychology, to help her understand people—and maybe herself.

At Quetzal hall, Valerie's roommate Ann seemed quite pleasant. She had a large face, and very thin penciled eyebrows over surprised looking eyes. She was kind-hearted, and also more sophisticated than Valerie, and had a tin of Constant Comment tea, which she made in a pot on the illegal hotplate that she had brought from home. It had an elegant taste of oranges and cinnamon to it, and Val felt she had learned something exotic that would help her to live as a poet should.

But alas, Ann was a smoker and liked to sneak a cigarette first thing in the morning, and a few more at bedtime, which caused Val to wheeze and cough, and have to use her inhaler during the night.

"It's strange," said Valerie. "I asked for a nonsmoking roommate, and they promised me."

"I'm sorry," said Ann. She stubbed out her cigarette in a tea saucer, and waved the smoke toward the window, even though it was closed. "I had to say I was a non-smoker because my Mom was helping with my application."

"She doesn't know you smoke?"

"No. She'd kill me! Please don't tell!"

"Okay," said Val. "Could you just try to smoke less in our room?"

"Sure," said Ann. "I'll do my best. And she did try. She got it down to only one cigarette at bedtime, and of course, one in the morning.

One evening Valerie was sitting on the sofa in the living room of Quetzal Hall, when she saw a tall girl come in through the front door—a girl about her own height, with shining, honey-colored hair, so much prettier than Val's rumpled, short brown hair. She walked swiftly through the room, and into the dorm office at the back. A little while later, the girl came out again, and sat down on the chair opposite Valerie, a worried look on her face.

"What happened?" Val asked her. She dared to ask, because the girl had such a kind, friendly face, and because she did look worried.

"Well, I just made a dumb mistake!" Her warm, rich voice seemed to hold laughter in it, even now when she was worried. "I just assumed there would be room for me here—I wrote to them last month and they didn't say no—and so I came in from L.A. on the bus. But now they say there's no room at all."

"Why don't you stay the night in my room?" said Val. We can ask for a roll-away bed, and I have an extra blanket and sheets. We can find a pillow easy."

"Really? Oh that would be wonderful! My name's Jo." She had the friendliest eyes, and the biggest smile Val thought she had ever seen.

"I'm Val. What fun!" she added. "We'll just have to check with my roommate, but I'm sure she'll say yes," Val stood up and, grabbing Jo's hand, gave her an encouraging tug as Jo stood up too. And there they were, friends for life.

The next day, Jo found a room for herself at a house about a mile from the college, and she told Valerie how there was a little attic room just on the other side of hers, that maybe Valerie could rent cheaply. All of a sudden, she was free of Quetzal Hall. The monthly allowance from her parents was just enough to rent the attic room, with a bit left over for food. It was the sweetest little room, with yellow-flowered wallpaper—tiny yellow flowers, like in a girl's sundress—and to get to it, you had to go through

Jo's room, which had a creamy-colored wallpaper, with bigger flowers on it—gardenias, maybe.

Mrs. Dennstedt was a kindly landlady, and allowed them to use the kitchen as much as they liked, except when she was preparing her own meals. There was a bathroom at the top of the stairs, just next to their rooms, and you could climb through the window onto a small deck for sunbathing. Sometimes, on a beautifully warm afternoon, they would dare to sunbathe naked, and giggled if a low-flying plane came by above them.

Val had just read *Great Expectations* in her English lit class, and Jo had read it a couple of years earlier. So they got in the habit of saying "What larks!" to each other, the way Pip and his kindly brother-in-law—who was also named Jo!—did in the novel. When Val was tucked away in her yellow-flowered attic room, she sometimes would slip notes under the door for Jo. "Okay to come through?"

And a note would glide back under the door, in Jo's rounded, first-grade teacher handwriting "All decent here!" Then Val would go prancing through in her bath towel and run for the shower.

"What larks!" Jo would call out as Val came dashing through again, her hair dripping wet.

Sometimes they would go to a little pizza parlor down the road, and order the very cheapest plain pizza. Jo would have a ten-cent can of mushrooms in her purse, and while they were waiting for the pizza, and the fraternity boys across the room were singing "Sweet Low, Sweet Chariot," Val would pull out of *her* purse the can opener from Mrs. Dennstedt's kitchen—and they would soon have a mushroom pizza for the price of a plain. It saved them a dollar, but most of all it was such fun, as they grinned at each other wickedly over their slices of pizza. "Swing Low, Sweet Chariot, Comin' for to carry me home!" sang the deep-voiced, drunken boys across the room.

Then Mrs. Dennstedt left them in charge of her house, and went away for a month in Europe. She was 82 years old, but she was intrepid and could travel to Europe on her own. Jo and Val admired her, and they tried to be good—but Jo was in her last year of Elementary Education and had been teaching kids to finger paint. What larks it would be to have a finger-painting party in Mrs. Dennstedt's garage. They spread a big oil cloth over the ping-pong table, and invited all their friends over. Fingers dipping into every color, sliding around on paper, and smearing the colors together—and of course glasses of beer, and everyone laughing. They hung the bright and smudgy paintings up with clothespins, on a line they strung above the ping-pong table.

Val had a boyfriend of sorts from the freshman quad—but she had fallen in love with Will, a tall, aloof fellow who was an art major, and she hoped he would be impressed by their painting party. He came by for a short while, and left behind an elegant piece, like Japanese calligraphy, that made all the other finger paintings look ridiculous and foolish. Val claimed it for herself, as soon as it had dried, and whisked it off to her room. He hadn't signed it, but at one spot where he had paused for a second, she could see his fingerprint.

She was thrilled when Will asked if he could paint her portrait. They would meet at the art studio at the college, and in the midst of the lovely smells of oil paint and linseed oil, he would gaze at her profile, and paint. They didn't talk much, because Will was concentrating. But they listened to records, and whenever a record came to an end, one of them would get up to turn it over, or put on a new one. Val liked folk music, but Will was into Bach, especially the Goldberg Variations. She loved learning how intricate and haunting that music is—especially with Glenn Gould playing—but she hoped Will wouldn't ask her to tell one variation from another.

The finger-painting party was momentous for another reason too; it was the beginning of the end of things. Max, a square-faced guy with a crew cut, who Jo had gone out with a few times, stood painting next to Valerie that night, and for some reason whispered in her ear: "You know, Jo is the first virgin I ever conquered."

With a flash of anger, Val wondered how many other people, how many guys, he had said that to. She turned away from him, and in her mind she scoffed at him because she knew Jo *wasn't* a virgin when she met him—but most of all, because she knew that Jo could never be conquered. Jo had first gone out with Max only because she had found his little brother playing on the lawn in front of Mrs. Dennstedt's, and she thought she would try out her new teaching skills on the surprised little boy.

They were having a grand time discussing salamanders and counting the legs on bugs, when his smiling big brother showed up, in a way that made him seem much nicer than he really was.

Something came of it all just the same. A few weeks after the finger-painting party, sitting on Val's bed in her attic hideaway, Jo told Val that somehow she had managed to become pregnant, and had to figure out what to do.

"What do you think of the situation?" she asked Val again—as if they were in a story, maybe an adventure story where all they had to do was solve the mystery.

"What do *you* think, Jo?" Val would reply, for she herself was bewildered and knew that whatever Jo did, she would handle it better than Val could ever manage to, if it happened to her. She knew that Jo was magical, and that whatever happened her life would be good.

"What do you think of the situation?" they would ask each other. And they would go over Jo's options. She could go home to her Mom's. She could stay right there at Mrs. Dennstedt's. She certainly could finish out her last year of teacher training, no matter how fast the baby grew.

"I would help you take care of the baby," said Val. "I would love your baby almost as much as you do." That was the one thing they knew for sure. Jo loved her baby from the moment she realized it was making its way to her.

It was for the baby's sake that Jo decided he or she should have a father, at least for a while. So she married Max and moved out of Mrs. Dennstedt's house and into an apartment with him. Val couldn't stand to be in her yellow-flowered attic room without Jo on the other side of the door.

As soon as she could, she found two roommates and moved into a flat on Acorn Street, a dead-end street that bumped right up against the College Drive-In movie theater. Val had gone there once with a football player she met in dance class, and she had to wrestle with him in the front seat of his car. It had been scary, and she had struggled fiercely against arms that muffled her breath, and hands that plunged, that grabbed her everywhere.

Then, suddenly it stopped. "I'll let you go this time," he said, in a princely way, "because I guess you really are a virgin." As if that had anything to do with it! Val hated him, and vowed to be more careful who she went out with. Only her friends! Only boys who wrote poetry!

Still, she was left with a horrible feeling about the drive-in. To live right next to it, she had to remind herself that just a couple of years earlier, she had gone there with her family—her little sister in pajamas in front with her parents, and she and her brother in back, sharing the popcorn, watching one of those singing cowboy movies. Not Roy Rogers but Gene Autry, the one who seemed real, the one she and her brother liked best.

Before long, Val got used to the idea of the drive-in, and came to love the apartment—her first grown-up apartment. She got along well with Cindy, one of the girls she shared it with. The other one, Deanna, kept stealing Val's carrots from the fridge, wrecking her attempts to diet, and they would have serious fights—over carrots! But Cindy was

Happy Holidays

This is a little book of stories that my mother wrote about her life as a young woman. We worked together to make this finished book. I hope you enjoy it.

– Rebecca

sweet and funny; she loved folk music, and would pour them all a glass of wine in the evenings, while they listened to Cynthia Gooding sing "Oh Waily Waily, but Love is bonny–a little while when it is new . . ."

She was almost starting to be happy there, when one day Will came by and showed her a painting of a hermit crab that he had just completed. It was a nicely done hermit crab, with vivid ochre and gold colors, outlined in black, in Will's unique style.

"I'm sorry," he said. "I just couldn't get your profile right, so I painted it over. You have such an odd nose," he explained. I shouldn't have tried a profile." Valerie knew he had done the profile because one of her eyes was a little crooked, but she was clever enough not to say so.

"I would have loved to have the painting just the same!" she protested. "It's probably the only time anyone will ever paint my portrait."

"Sorry, I never thought of that," he said in his aloof but somehow winsome way. He himself had a beautiful profile that she loved gazing at–the way his nose lifted a little just at the tip, and the long lashes of his eyes. "And besides, I needed the canvas."

He painted her over with a hermit crab! Because he needed the canvas! If that wasn't a message, she supposed there never would be one. "What larks!" she told herself, and wished Jo was there to laugh with her.

But Jo and her sweet baby girl had moved back home to her Mom's in L.A. after Max failed to love Jo, or even that dear baby. Now Jo was teaching second grade, and hatching baby chicks in her classroom, just as she always wanted to. Val hardly ever got to see Jo any more, but when she did, she would say to Jo, "What do you think of the situation?" And they would smile at each other, and sometimes even have a good laugh about it. And Jo seemed happy, in love with her baby, in love with teaching, and just at the beginning of her new life.

Since the flat on Acorn Street was right at the edge of the drive-in theater's back fence, Val and her new roommates and their friends liked to go out in the back yard after dinner and look up at the big screen, with the rows of cars spread out beneath it. They would stand there with their sweaters and jackets on against the chill of evening, and gaze across the cyclone fencing. They could watch giant close-ups of beautiful people kissing, and sometimes they could figure out the stories. What they hadn't figured out was how to get hold of the little metal radios that hung inside the paying customers' car windows, and made things sound so tinny—even the most romantic voices, even the music.

A RED JEEP

I. Desert Adventure

Since Jordan lived right upstairs from Val and Cindy's apartment, they could hear him shuffling around above them at 5 a.m., and noisier than usual, with a few loud thumps to be sure they were up. Way too soon, he tapped on their door. There he was, with that rumpled sandy hair of his, and a sleepy-eyed grin. "Ready?"

"Almost," Val said, and yelled to Cindy who was still in the bathroom. She emerged with her blond pageboy shining, while Val had barely managed a brush through her own short brown hair, nearly as rumpled as Jordy's.

"First let me feed Indigo." Jordy pulled two mice by their tails from his pocket, lifted the cover of the glass aquarium where the Indigo snake lived, and dropped them in. Having a pet snake in their living room made Val and Cindy seem very cool whenever they had a party—but they couldn't have managed it if Jordy didn't take care of the food supply. Indigo perked up immediately when the mice dropped in. He began to slither about, playing a bit with his breakfast, the way a cat does. True to his name, Indigo was a dark blue-black color—a lithe and beautiful creature—and his yellow eyes glowed intelligently.

Watching him did wonders for waking them up.

"Okay, shall we go now?" Val grabbed the bag of sandwiches she had made the night before, and the thermos of hot tea. The three of them walked to Jordy's battered red jeep. As she and Cindy climbed into the stiff little back seat, Val was glad to see that Jordy had fastened the canvas roof and sides on, to make it as snug as possible for the trek over the San Diego Mountains—which would be plenty cold. The front seat stayed empty for Mike, as they drove to pick him up. Unlike the rest of them, Mike still lived at home with his parents and his childhood pet, an aged dog named Pandy. He and Jordy were completely different from each other—but they'd been best friends since they were both outsiders in seventh grade.

What Valerie liked best about Mike was that, just like her, he wanted to be a writer. And she liked how he loved his old dog Pandy. And he could be very funny. When she sat out on the lawn for the hour between Abnormal Psych and her Creative Writing class, he would sit down beside her and draw cartoons in her class notes. A little stick figure with the word "Psycho!" in the margin of her psychology lecture notes, for instance. What she didn't like was the way he squashed bugs just to make her cringe; and the time he stole the Irish grammar she had sent away to Ireland for, to learn the language of Irish poets—then never gave it back.

Truth be told, Mike's greatest asset was that his parents had given him a 1923 Plymouth with a rumble seat. Sometimes Jordy would drive, with Val's friend Cindy in the front seat beside him, just so Val and Mike could cuddle in the rumble seat late at night, as the little Plymouth went zooming around the Mission Valley highway, and down to the roaring, glittering ocean. Val and Cindy were what they called "nice girls" in those days, and Mike and Jordy were nice boys. All of them were virgins. The girls, at least, understood that they should stay that way until they got married (though Cindy was beginning to have doubts) and the boys were too nice to suggest otherwise.

But it was the boys who had the cars. The only girl Val knew of who had a car was Nancy Drew, in *The Adventures of Nancy Drew* that she used to read in high school. Nancy Drew had a little blue roadster that Valerie loved to imagine driving. But in real life, no girls she knew had parents who would buy them a car. It bothered her, but there it was. So there were three vehicles of adventure: a red jeep, an old white Plymouth with a rumble seat, and a little blue roadster. The one owned by a girl was imaginary; the Plymouth was fun and almost romantic. But it was the little red jeep that took them on actual adventures.

The adventures were courtesy of Jordy's job at the Natural History Museum in Balboa Park. He was a senior, class of 1956—a year ahead of the rest of them—and he already had a full-time job lined up at the Museum the minute he graduated in June, if the draft didn't get him first. The draft hovered over all of Val's male friends, and she worried about them because they were none of them cut out for the army. How could they be? It didn't seem fair that she should be safe and they not.

There was an early morning silence among them in the jeep as they drove to Mike's house; it was still dark when they picked him up.

"Where's my Irish grammar?" Val demanded, as soon as he was settled into the front seat. "I need my Irish grammar!"

Mike chuckled in that fake nasal chuckle of his. "Can't think what you're talking about."

"Can't think why you put up with him," said Cindy in her best wise-cracking voice.

"I hope you guys dressed warm," Jordy broke in. "It's going to be extra cold in the mountains this morning."

Crossing the San Diego mountains was always the biggest challenge, especially in the back seat. The canvas roof and sides that Jordy had snapped on had some thin see-through plastic panels in them that were no protection at all against the cold. Val and Cindy leaned into each other, shivering and laughing themselves warm as best they could while the jeep climbed higher. And then came the wonderful downhill part, with Jordy letting the jeep take its own reins. Down they sped, as the sun rose on the desert. Glorious change! There were the sand dunes, shifting and changing with every hour of the day, every glance of the sun—and yet golden and gleaming, changeless and eternal. No one said a word when they first came into the dunes. There was always a silence at first—the way birds are silent just at the moment of sunrise.

Then they shook their heads, laughed a bit, and tooled along the desert slowly until Jordy spied a rattlesnake. He stopped the jeep, jumped out with a drawstring cloth bag in his left hand, and grabbed the snake just behind its head with a deft right hand, while it rattled like crazy. He placed it firmly in the bag, pulled the drawstring tight, tied one knot in it, and tossed it in the back section–just behind Val and Cindy. Val felt a little chill between her shoulder blades, but she trusted Jordy's knot.

Next thing he found was a sweet little horned toad, who they all admired and let sit on their hands. Val loved the feel of his soft, bumpy skin and his tiny pulsing heartbeat under her fingers. He almost seemed to *want* to come with them. But into another cloth bag he went. And the same with the trapdoor spider Jordy found near a burnished, maroon manzanita bush. He dug up the whole clump of sand around it, moistened it a bit with drops from their drinking water to keep it together, and placed it in a small jar with a perforated lid, one of Jordy's neat little row of collecting jars in a sturdy wooden frame, just behind the back seat.

By noon they could all declare the expedition a success. Jordy stopped the jeep at a desert bodega for some tacos and beer. It had appeared like a mirage for hallucinating travelers. Never mind the sandwiches! Under the sun-bleached frame and palm-branch awning of the outdoor eating area, they grinned at one another.

"How could Jordy manage without us?" said Val. "Never could manage," said Jordy.

II. Balboa Park

Valerie had some peculiar jobs while working her way through San Diego State, Class of '57. For a while she climbed the stairs to the dingy downtown office of the AFL/CIO Newsletter, and wrote pro-union articles that, to her parents' horror, turned her into a defiant Democrat. Then, for another while, she rode in carpools all the way out to the Navy Electronics Lab on Point Loma, where she ran peculiar long square-sided pins through designated holes in those newfangled IBM cards for the Lab's big mainframe computer; and where she also had a crush on a kind, middle-aged man who pretended not to notice.

But the most fun job was the one Jordy got for her at the Museum of Natural History in Balboa Park. The Museum was in one of those grand old Spanish style buildings that dated from the big exposition in 1935, the year Valerie was born. Val would take the city bus to Balboa Park on Sundays, bringing a sandwich for lunch. The job didn't start until one, but she loved sitting on the grass beneath the tall palm trees, munching her sandwich and feeling the warm breezes of that gentle place.

The Museum of Natural History looked exotic from the outside, with its red tile roof, ivory stucco walls, and wrought iron grills on the windows. But inside it was dull and dusty, and seemed to be crumbling away, little piles of plaster in the corners and on the window sills. Once Val saw a little murex shell lying on one of those window sills, its outer white spikes almost as dusty as the sill, its inner pink spiral all shining like nail polish—and she slipped it into the pocket of her skirt. In a moment of conscience, she showed it to Jordy later on.

"Sure, keep it," he said. "It's probably one that I brought in anyway."

This made sense; Jordy was the main source of a big chunk of the museum's marine collection. He loved catching nudibranchs in the tide pools of Baja California, and had contributed a variety of live ones to the museum's aquarium. If it wasn't for Jordy, Val would never even have heard of nudibranchs, though she might have known them by their other name—sea slugs. But once you learned it, nudibranch was a much better name for them, for they were colorful and mysterious little creatures, with more colors and patterns than you could possibly find in flowers, or even in precious jewels—like the iridescent purple one with waving orange tendrils all along its back, or the black one with vivid emerald stripes that seemed to glow like the radium watches that some people wore so they could tell time in the dark.

Val was in awe of Jordy's knowledge of nudibranchs. But she couldn't help feeling there was a loftier purpose in being an English major and knowing who the great poets were. She could chant Keats's "Ode on Melancholy" almost all the way through from memory, though she hadn't found anyone who would listen past the first line without breaking into laughter. So she had to turn it into a joke. "No, no go not to Lethe!" with a hand comically over her brow. Betraying Keats for a little laughter. Who would do that?

But being an English major would not help her much in her job at the Natural History Museum. The job was to run a film projector on Sunday afternoons, showing nature documentaries to old people, and she was afraid of getting Jordy into trouble because of her mechanical incompetence.

"What if I break the projector?"

"You'll be fine," Jordy said. "Besides, I'm just down the hall, and I can always fix it."

The projector was set up at the center of the aisle in the back of the room, and Val's hands would be shaking as she tried to steady the machine when it began stuttering. It sounded like the noise a bicycle makes when you stick a playing card to one of the spokes, the way Val and her brother used to do, pretending their bikes had motors. Jordy taught her how to splice the film with a piece of tape whenever it broke—as it often did. The Museum of Natural History had no idea what a patchwork its film archive was becoming. There were at least a dozen clumsy splices in the two reels of *The Living Desert*, and almost as many in *Seal Island*. And even though her hands were shaking when she tried to fix the broken film, the old people were sweet to her as she walked up the aisle to introduce the films each Sunday. They were very patient whenever the film broke, and would just chuckle in a friendly way.

This Sunday Val was especially shaky because she had just broken up with Mike. There had always been those things that she didn't really like about him—like stepping on bugs or stealing her Irish grammar—but he was the only boyfriend she'd ever had, and she felt attached to him. And now she was devastated because last night he told her that he had fallen in love with a tall girl name Lorna, who had curly platinum blond hair in a poodle cut all over the top of her head.

"She is like a giant vanilla ice cream cone," he explained. "And she is very funny."

"But I'm funny too," Val said.

"Yes, but you are old funny," Mike said, "and she is new funny." He grinned and seemed to think that was quite amusing too.

Valerie didn't think there was anything funny about a giant vanilla ice cream cone destroying her life. Like a giant vanilla Godzilla, she thought, and she knew if she said it out loud someone would think it was funny. And for that very reason she kept it to herself, where it could be horribly sad.

So this Sunday her hands were shaking worse than ever, and she couldn't even thread the first reel of *The Vanishing Prairie*. She ran down the hall and asked Jordy to help her. "I can't do it, I can't do it!" she cried.

"I know," he said. "Mike told me. It's okay. You go on home if you want, or stay right here. I'll do the movie for you."

"No, I'll do it myself," she said firmly. "If you just start the machine, I'll do the rest."

"Giant Vanilla Godzilla," she said as they walked down the echoing hall, back to the projection room.

"What?" Jordy looked at her with a puzzled grin. "Is that today's movie?"

"It is for me," she said. And sure enough, in the second reel there was a fight to the death between a tarantula and a scorpion that could give anyone bad dreams.

III. Fraternity Dance

"Why don't you come to my fraternity dance?" Jordy asked her as they rode home together. "I don't have a date yet, and there's a good band."

"Sure," she said. She knew he was asking just to make her feel better about Mike. But it did make her feel better. Jordy's fraternity had a bad reputation, but he hadn't known that when he pledged. He only did it because he thought it would help him with his shyness. And they only asked him because he was a scientist and knew how to make alcohol that was somewhat safe to drink.

Since Jordy lived right upstairs, he picked Val up without much fanfare. But in deference to the occasion, he didn't have any mice in his pockets and didn't try to feed Indigo.

He had on a beige sport jacket that was a just little too big, and a funny green bow tie that somehow suited him. His sandy hair was combed neatly, and he had a sweet broad grin on his face. "You look nice," he said. She was wearing her black polka-dot dress with the big swingy skirt and the white shawl collar that dipped down in back, and she knew that she looked pretty in it. It was her only dress that she hadn't made herself, and practically the only one that didn't have a lumpy waistline or a crooked hem.

"You look nice too," she said. Val felt surprisingly happy to see him, and almost skipped beside him out to the jeep.

"We have to stop at the lab first," he told her. "I have to pick up the alcohol."

"Oh yeah," she grinned. "I forgot you are the chemist. You know, I've never been to a fraternity dance before."

"Well, it's nothing special," he said. "Except tonight they have that good band I told you about. I heard them when we first hired them. Really good swing music!"

Val was nervous about dancing, because she wasn't very good at it. But fortunately, she'd taken a ballroom dancing class for her gym requirement.

The fraternity had hired a ballroom in an old hotel downtown. Val knew her mom wouldn't like the sound of that, but she felt safe with Jordy. There were square brown pillars with gold edging, and brown carpeting—nothing too festive or fancy. But the fraternity boys and their sorority girlfriends had hung bright balloons everywhere. And the big dance floor was shiny as a skating rink.

Jordy's fraternity brothers greeted him with welcoming smiles as they saw the two jugs in his hands.

"Hey, Jordy! How much did you bring?"

"Couple more," he said. "They're out in my jeep if someone wants to get them."

He dropped the jugs behind the bar, and then fixed drinks for himself and Val in two paper cups, mixing some ginger ale with his home-made alcohol. "Come on," he said. "Let's go sit down with these."

They found a little table, just for the two of them, and Val was grateful that he wasn't asking her to talk to the fraternity brothers and their sorority girlfriends. The girls were all wearing pastel-colored angora sweaters and woolen circle skirts, and looked askance at her polka-dot dress. But for once, Val didn't care. She sipped her drink and smiled at Jordy. The music was loud and happy. Elvis Presley's "Blue Suede Shoes" was big that year, and she couldn't help loving it, even though she and Cindy were more into folk songs. Then the band began playing an old jitterbug tune, and Jordy said, "I dare you!"

"I'm not such a good dancer," she told him.

"Neither am I," he laughed. "But I bet we are tipsy enough for this one!"

"I kinda learned the Lindy in dance class," she admitted. "It's so much more fun than—"

"Show me," he said. "You can lead if you want."

"Oh, sure," she laughed. But she started moving, and then Jordy was moving with her, and the whole room was swinging around them. Oh, *this* was dancing! This was dancing! They were smiling broadly at each other, and every time he twirled her around, their eyes met when she twirled back again. He held up his arm and she twirled so lightly, like a ballerina, and then they came together again and dipped and pranced and swayed with joy and abandon.

"I thought you said you couldn't dance!" he laughed, when the music stopped.

"I thought you said *you* couldn't!"

IV. Tide Pools

They often went together to the tide pools in La Jolla, where she helped Jordy look for interesting creatures. She never thought of Jordy as her boyfriend, and he never said anything about it either. But they loved careening through Mission Valley together after dark, after a swim and a tide pool adventure. How happily the little red jeep would swing along the smooth and winding road with stars above them, and the headlight beams just ahead. How snug and safe and adventurous they felt together.

This time there were no nudibranchs—but they found a perfect sand dollar, and a beautiful starfish.

"We don't need these," said Jordy. "Let's leave them here, like you and me."

"Leave us here?"

"Well, you are going away so soon," he said.

It was true. She was going away to the University of Chicago, where she was going to get a master's degree in Psychology. Her parents were willing to pay for something more practical than English, and she thought it might be useful anyway, if she still became a writer. But she hadn't thought about whether it would matter to Jordy. "Okay," she said. "Let's leave us here."

And that's what they did. She didn't even look back. She didn't even wonder why.